Acknowledgments
We would like to express our thanks to UNUMA,
the Civil Society in Support of Indigenous People,
and especially to the Carreño family of the village of
Cachama, state of Anzoátegui, for their help and
collaboration in the creation of this book.

Text copyright © 1998 by María Elena Maggi
Illustrations copyright © 1998 by Gloria Calderón
English language translation copyright © 2001 by Elisa Amado
Originally published in Spanish as *La gran canoa*
by Playco Editores, Venezuela, © 1998

Groundwood Books / Douglas & McIntyre
720 Bathurst Street, Suite 500, Toronto, Ontario M5S 2R4

Distributed in the USA by Publishers Group West
1700 Fourth Street, Berkeley, CA 94710

We acknowledge the financial support of the Canada Council for the
Arts, the Ontario Arts Council and the Government of Canada
through the Book Publishing Industry Development Program for our
publishing activities.

National Library of Canada Cataloguing in Publication Data
Maggi, María Elena
The great canoe
Translation of : La gran canoa.
"A Groundwood book"
ISBN 0-88899-444-3
1. Carib Indians — Folklore. 2. Deluge — Folklore. I. Calderón,
Gloria. II. Amado, Elisa. III. Title.
PZ8.1.M353Gr 2001   j398.2'089'984   C2001-930639-3

Printed and bound in China by Everbest Printing Co. Ltd.

THE GREAT CANOE

A KARIÑA LEGEND RETOLD BY

MARÍA ELENA MAGGI

ILLUSTRATED BY

GLORIA CALDERÓN

Translated by Elisa Amado

•

A GROUNDWOOD BOOK
DOUGLAS & McINTYRE
TORONTO VANCOUVER BUFFALO

A very long time ago,

Kaputano, the Sky Dweller, arrived in the land of the Kariña people.

"Listen, my children," he said. "I have come to tell you that a great rain will soon begin to fall and that the world will be completely covered by water."

But of the people gathered there, only four couples were afraid when they heard his words. The rest did not believe him.

"I am the father of the Kariña," he insisted, "and I don't want my children to die. Help me to build a canoe that will hold us all. That way we won't drown."

"You aren't our father. Nothing is going to happen," said the people, except for the four couples who were scared half to death.

"You will see," said Kaputano.

Then the four couples went to work and helped
Kaputano to build a very large canoe.

When they had finished, they gathered together
two of each kind of animal and herded them onto
the canoe.

They also brought a seed from each kind of plant.

Just as they finished loading the canoe, the sky
turned as dark as night.

And it rained without stopping for many days.

The rivers overflowed. There was so much water that animals were swept away and you could no longer see the tops of even the tallest trees.

The Kariña who had stayed behind could not be rescued because the waves were too high. Their world was drowned in water.

Days later when the waters went down and the land was dry again, Kaputano asked the survivors, "How do you want the world to be, as you see it now?"

But the Kariña said that no people could live
in a place like this.

"Where are the groves of palms whose
leaves we weave into baskets and roofs?"

"Where are the mountains on whose slopes we grow food?"

"Where are the rivers in which we can fish?"

"And where are the trees that shelter us?"

It was then that Kaputano created a new world for his
children, the Kariña — a world rich with marshes, rivers,
mountains and many trees.

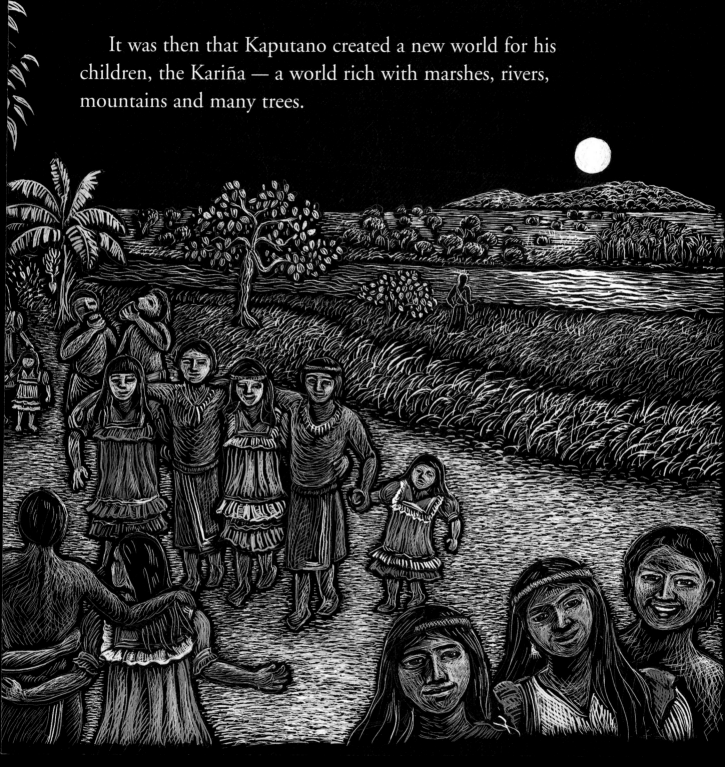

AFTERWORD

THE KARIÑA are the descendants of a great indigenous nation that, before the Spaniards came, occupied eastern Venezuela from the Orinoco River to the northern coast, including some islands in the Caribbean. Great sailors, traders and warriors, they fiercely resisted the invader, who called them the Carib Indians.

Today the majority of these people live in the eastern grasslands of the states of Anzoátegui, northern Bolívar, and Monagas and Sucre.

According to their myths and legends, the ancestors of the Kariña were created from the bones of a great snake. In pre-Columbian days they lived in large round houses called *caneyes,* which are roofed with the leaves of a palm called *moriche.* They ate, received guests and held feasts in their houses, although they also had an even larger hut where they could celebrate community events.

During the past few decades, the Kariña way of life has changed due to more contact with non-native people and to oil exploration in the Anzoátegui region. Nonetheless many Kariña retain their language and ancestral culture. Today, many still live from hunting, fishing, gathering and farming, which is carried on communally on their *conucos* (communal lands) and in their *morichales* (palm groves). Among their foods are *cassava* (yucca cakes) and *cachiri* (liquor made from yucca root). With fiber from the *moriches* they weave nets, baskets and ornaments. While now they live in houses made from cement blocks, they still build their traditional *caneyes* beside or behind their houses. This is where they hold their feasts. An important day is Akaatommpo, celebrated on November 2, the Day of the Dead, when the Kariña dance *maremare* to music made by pan flutes and a little drum they call a *sampura.* This dance is shown in the last illustration of the book.

THE IDEA for this book came from a long-standing interest in seeing the universal story of Noah's Ark set in the New World. When I discovered that there was in fact a Kariña version, which I found in Fray Cesáreo de Armellada's book, *Indigenous Venezuelan Literatures*, it seemed like the ideal basis for a retelling of the story. Extensive research revealed that anthropologist Marc de Civrieux's *Religion and Kariña Magic* contained versions of the same story. I researched the flora and fauna found in Anzoátegui and Bolívar states and along the banks of the Orinoco River. Finally the illustrator, Gloria Calderón, and I went to visit the Kariña in Cachama, Cerro Negro, Las Pocotas and Tascabeña, staying with members of the Carreño family, who are leaders in these communities. We also spoke to other leaders with whom we drank *cachiri* and listened to *maremare*. These encounters deepened our commitment to transmit the stories of the Kariña people and their physical world as accurately as possible.

The text was rewritten once the illustrations were complete to make it as short as possible. Its structure follows Fray Cesáreo de Armellada's, drawing on two of his stories — "The Great Canoe" and "The World Cannot Be the Same." His third story on the origins of work was omitted. Elements are also drawn from Marc de Civrieux's account, including the name of the god Kaputano and the emphasis on the punishment of non-believers. Though this might seem a bit harsh for children, Civrieux considered it an essential element in Kariña religion. Thus, although the story is universal, here it is told in the very particular way it is known to the Kariña.